This Faber book belongs to

....

To Mum and Dad, with all my love.
C.R.

First published in the UK in 2016
by Faber and Faber Ltd,
Bloomsbury House,
74–77 Great Russell Street, London WC1B 3DA

The text was first published as the poem 'Summer Evening'
in Walter de la Mare's *Peacock Pie* poetry collection in 1913.

Printed in China

Text © The Literary Trustees of Walter de la Mare, 1969
Illustrations © Carolina Rabei, 2016

A CIP record for this book is available
from the British Library

HB ISBN 978–0–571–31466–9
PB ISBN 978–0–571–31467–6

10 9 8 7 6 5 4 3 2 1

MIX
Paper from
responsible sources
FSC® C005748

❊ A FABER PICTURE BOOK ❊

Summer Evening

Walter de la Mare
illustrated by Carolina Rabei

ff

FABER & FABER

The sandy cat by the Farmer's chair

Mews at his knee for dainty fare;

Old Rover in his moss-greened house

Mumbles a bone,

and barks at a mouse.

In the dewy fields the cattle lie

Chewing the cud 'neath a fading sky;

Dobbin at manger pulls his hay:

Gone is another summer's day.